W9-DIB-414

moose n' me

by

Kenny Loggins

with pictures by Joshua Nash

Thank You...

Steve Moir, Gary Borman, Melinda Williams, Eva Ein, Chris Burke and Eric Custer

Special Thanks To....

Joshua Nash for your talented input and endless patience

Hana Loggins for your discerning eye

Jimmy Messina for always believing in Moose

Scott Bernard for helping me bring Moose home

And Angie Bazzana for all your creativity and guidance

This Book is Dedicated To...

Crosby, Cody, Bella, Luke and Hana. I wish Moose could have known you too.

– Pops

Foreword

There's always one dog. One special dog you'll never forget. One dog that touched your heart in a way that lasts a lifetime. For me, that dog was Moose.

As I reached into the puppy pen, I picked him out 'cause he was the fattest, the first-to-the-bowl puppy, the "moose" of the litter. Or maybe he picked me, 'cause he was the first of the pack to say "hi", lick my hand and look into my eyes. It was sort'a like meeting an old friend for the first time.

And we would stay best friends for 14 years, through my youth and transition into half of the duo, "Loggins and Messina". Interesting, transformational times.

Actually, I started the song, "Moose n' Me", just before I met Jimmy Messina, 1970, and even though Jim always liked the song, I never recorded it back then because I always figured it wasn't quite done yet. Something was missing. I wanted my song about Ol' Moose to be a little bit more, just like him. I figured it needed "seasoning". Or should I say, I did?

Cut to 30-some years later. I'd been working on a new "Family CD" called "All Join In", and I had recorded most of the CD when I realized I needed to write a song of my own for this very special collection of favorite songs. Something fun, something heartful, something whimsical. Not as easy as it sounds.

One morning I woke up with a melody I almost didn't recognize at first, swirling in my head. There it was, "Moose is a good dog, a good dog Moosie is." A melody from my own childhood, 30 years forgotten. And suddenly I knew how that last verse should go.

Still, I was surprised and a bit stunned by what came out. I felt a sadness I hadn't really let myself feel in a very long time, my own remorse over having been on the road when Ol' Moose had passed on. Then that bridge and last verse poured out, as if it was a way for Moose to tell me it was all OK, and we'd meet up again when the time was right.

I'd read somewhere about a "near death experience," where the person who "died" was met at the "Pearly Gates" by her beloved dog before any angels or relations met her, and I was struck with the calm, no doubt assuredness that Moose would be the first one there for me too.

Ironically, at the same time that I wrote the new last verse, my son, Luke, and daughter, Hana lost their beloved Border Collie of 14 years, Sprocket. It was a rough passage for them all, and I realized that "Moose n' Me" had an important message for them too. There IS a better place we ALL get to go, not just humans, and it's comforting to know that some day we will all meet again up there.

I then decided that this simple little "children's song" should become a book too, and I offer it to those parents struggling to find a way to console a distraught child who may have lost that closest of all best friends, the beloved pet. I sincerely hope this will make the tears ease a little sooner and bring a smile to all your faces.

— Kenny Loggins

Me and Moose were heading down the river,
makin' for the Delta line.

All our friends were back up in the mountains
where me and Moosie had spent our lives.

Pappy say "no lazy hound dog is ever gonna
stray from where he's born".

But Moose is crazy —
Moosie thinks that I'm his home.

Captain Ferguson was waitin' by the river,
where me and Moose had planned to stay.

But before Cap n' I could make a connection
some fella' said I was in his way.

He came at me with a crazy-eyed stagger,
but the Moose just growled him down.

And I smiled and whispered
as my foe turned around…

Moose, you're a good dog.

Moose is a good dog.

Moose is a good dog.

And I'd like to say
a good dog Moosie is.

Backroads and highways, so go the years.

And a young man must follow his dreams,
but hearts stay connected wherever they roam.

One night, miles away,
somethin' told me he was gone.

People talk a' how we'll all be reunited
when we pass through the Pearly Gates.

Mom and Dad and Bob are gonna make it
n' you can bet we're gonna celebrate.

We all believe we'll be meetin' our maker
when it's long past time to spare.

(But if) His angels can't make it,
I know the one who'll meet me there.

Moose, is a good dog.

Moose is a good dog.

Moose is a good dog.

And I'd like to say
a good dog Moosie is.

Text by Kenny Loggins (from lyrics to the song "Moose n' Me" © 2009 Universal Music Corp.)
Illustrations by Joshua Nash © 2011 Good Ol' Dog Publishing

Published by Good Ol' Dog Publishing
1187 Coast Village Rd Suite 1-140
Santa Barbara, CA 93108

ISBN 978-0-578-07552-5
Library of Congress Control Number: 2010942649

Printed in the U.S.A. by CreativeBeans

Buyers of Moose n' Me have the confidence of knowing they support responsible forest management. The Sterling Gloss paper used in the book's printing carries three chain-of-custody certifications:

Forest Stewardship Council
(FSC), BV-COC-953662; "The Independent Assurance for Responsible Forest Management."

Sustainable Forestry Initiative
(SFI), BV-SFICOC-US09000011; "Good for you. Good for our forests."

Programme for the Endorsement of Forest Certification
(PEFC), PEFC/29-31-12; "Promoting sustainable forest management."

To hear the classic "Moose n' Me" song and other Kenny Loggins music, log on to

www.kennyloggins.com

Visit the "Kid's Only" section on Kenny's website for fun downloadable activities for families to enjoy together!

Kenny Loggins

Singer-songwriter-author, Kenny Loggins has sold over 25 million albums worldwide, is the recipient of two Grammy Awards and has also co-written the book, *The Unimaginable Life, Lessons Learned on the Path of Love*. In addition to his string of successful singles and albums, both solo and as a member of the famed duo, Loggins & Messina, Kenny became the first major rock star to dedicate himself to also recording music for children/families. His album, *Return To Pooh Corner*, is still the best selling children's album of the last 20 years. Kenny currently resides in Santa Barbara, CA with his youngest children, and continues to write and record music for both adults and children alike.

Joshua Nash

Joshua has been a graphic artist for over a decade and illustrating professionally since 2004. He has had the pleasure of working with a range of wonderful clients including Scholastic Books and Hooked on Phonics. He enjoys a quiet life in Roseville, CA, where he lives with his wife, dog and cat.